MY THIRTY SHORT STORIES

SANJIT PAL

To the sacred memory of —

1. Late Kalipada Pal (My beloved grandfather)

2. Late Chapala Pal (My beloved grandmother)

3. Late Tushta Ranjan Pal (My beloved maternal grand

father)

4. Late Kanaklata Pal (My beloved maternal grand

mother)

5. Late Mukunda Pal (My beloved maternal uncle)

6. Late Shankar Prasad Sarkar (My beloved father-

in-law)

Contents

Contents

Preface

It is a matter of pleasure and pride for me to assert that I am going to publish my book titled "My Thirty Short Stories". My book contains diverse themes like social issues, didactic lessons, separation in relationship, hilarious touches, tragic elements, autobiographical touches, unacceptable love and so on.
This is not a collection of stories meant solely for young minds,it is a treasure trove for anyone seeking a glimpse into the depths of human emotions.
May the readers find solace, laughter, inspiration unfurling the pages.
I hope that more and more readers will praise the technique of my story -telling.I express my gratitude to the publisher.

Sanjit Pal
The Author

Kalyani,
Dist.Nadia
7th July,2024

CHAPTER ONE

A Hilarious Tale of Monkeys

I used to dwell at Nabadwip, a holy place. My early schooling was there. Ours was a joint family. My family consisted of my father, mother, sisters, brothers, grandfather, grandmother, uncle, aunt and so on.

Gone are those days. I lived on the bank of the river Bhagirathi. The ancestral house where I spent my boyhood really reckons me. There was a great banyan tree there and there was a Shiva Temple beneath the big trees. Any one can find out this location even to day. The place was noted for its monkeys. As it is a pilgrimage, many people come here everyday. They threw food at the monkeys. A troop of monkeys always used to move to and fro. But the inhabitants of this town did not mind it.

I recall some hilarious incidents pertaining to monkeys. One day when I was a student of Class IX or X, I was preparing my lessons in the day time. Our two storied house and jute godown were side by side. My grandmother Mrs. Chapala Pal kept a strict vigil on the 'Bari', which she spread on the roof in the broad day light of the sun to dry. Perhaps it was winter. At that very moment, a monkey came to my grandmother and started to shake her head. My grandmother called out, "Save me, save me." She was crying bitterly. Then I rushed there to rescue her from the plunk of monkeys.

I am going to tell you a tale of another funny incident. I was getting down from the upstairs. Then I became perplexed to see a group of monkeys coming from the room with potatoes in the mouths and hands of monkeys. They dipped their heads into the pots of our atta flour. Their faces turned into white. Taking a jar of biscuits from out neighbouring areas was a common phenamenon.

Another incident that took place was really deserves to be mentioned. Perhaps I was a young man of nearly 25 years old. I was going to the Ganges to take a bath in the river. At that time I was passing through a narrow alley. I did not know how and when a monkey came from behind me. It gave a slap on my hip. I cried, "Who?" I found that the naughty monkey who made its path to proceed on.

In the year 2012 I went to Mumbai in the month of October with my wife, Lipika and my son, Sovan. By the streamer I was going to see the Elephanta Cave. After reaching there I was ascending from the launch. There were some foreigners, too. All on a sudden, a monkey snatched away a bottle of colddrinks which the foreigner was holding. The funny sight was that the monkey started to drink after opening the lid of the bottle. Really, such sorts of funny incidents are still vivid in my memory and I will cherish them throughout my life.

CHAPTER TWO

THE DISCORD OF A GOLDEN FAMILY

They must have slept for almost nine years together. They passed their life in glee. They used to stay in a small town. Their marriage was an arranged marriage. They referred to Surojit and Sumitra. They had a super cute son named Raju. There was a gloomy tale regarding their break-up of relationship. Many a man wept for their separation. Had Soma any regret ? Who knew ?

There was a feeling of happiness in their relationship. After the passing of five years of their wedding, an atmosphere of mistrust was going on to occur. Indeed it was one of the bad impacts of social media. It was heard that Sumitra, the wife of Surojit had had an affair with the neighbour of her in-laws. Everything became normal after a period of time. It was true that the husband loved his wife dearly. Their beloved son Raju was admitted to a private English Medium School. The family was financially well-off. The members of the family went to restaurant to have supper whenever possible. They paid a visit to several tourist spots together.

Suspicion led to doom. Sumitra often lost temper. Under such circumstances she went to her parents intentionally. This sort of process was going on frequently. None believed what was behind it. Such was continuing.

Her husband went to her father-in-laws's house to bring back his agitated wife. But there was no positive answer. The husband waited for her. No doubt, there was a cry of despair. Oneday a person known to her husband called Surojit over phone, "Do you know the news ? What news ? Your wife is missing."

A rumour spread that Sumitra had an illicit love affair with a man who lived in the village where the girl's parents dwelt. The man was a daily wage earner and his house was an earthen one. How a bonding split over nothingless except passonate love which was the contribution of the bad influence of a mobile phone! It was a hearsay that Sumitra used to eat, to sleep, to do domestic work taking her phone always with her. She was indifferent to the well-being of her own son. A well wisher of Surojit told, "Is it possible ? Can an animal do it ?"

When the exact news came, it was known to all that Sumitra had eloped with her lover i.e. with that poor man leaving her luxury. Not only that, she did it without thinking of her son, Raju. She did not leave her husband but also she left her son for the sake of love. She only thought of self-contentment. Really, it seemed unbearable.
But it was a true fact and her husband became crazy. The boy lost her mother perpectually. Now he despises his mother. But the husband of Sumitra is still lamenting for her love. It is the epitome of social decay. Both father and son have lost their words to ventilate feelings to the entire

world.

CHAPTER THREE

THE AGONY OF AN OLD WOMAN

The old woman always found herself to be ill-fated. Since the dawn of her wedding, she had been unlucky. When she was pregnant, she lost her beloved husband. She prayed to the Almighty that she might be blessed with a son. Perhaps the Almighty listened to her fervent appeal. Really, it was the gift of the Almighty. A son was born to her. After losing her hasband, she pined. By dint of her hard toil, she somehow managed her family doing domestic work to others' houses. In this way, she brought her son up with difficulty.

Years passed by. She had a little hut of her own. But it was a matter of sorrow that she had no right to stay there. She had to live miserably. When her son grew up he was married to a beautiful lady. The economic condition of the son was not sufficient. The name of the man was Banamali who earned his livelihood by singing devotional songs. The man had to spend time leaving the small cottage. The man had two sons named Radhamadhab and Ranjit. The daughter-in-law of the old woman behaved with her mother-in-law badly.

The pangs of the old woman were intolerable. Her hair became white. Her sari was tattered, she started to beg in order to make both ends meet. The old woman had no where to go. But the irony was that the old woman was scared of storms. Whenever the sky was overcast with cloud, she took shelter in nearby pucca houses. Thus, the days went on in distress.

The old woman reached the evening stage of her life. Her death was too tragic to tell.

One day her daughter-in-law said "Leave from here." The infirm woman began to weep bitterly. Her grandson was good. He took pity on his grandmother. He convinced his mother. But it was all in vain. Her grandson had not completed his graduation till then. He was needy, too. He was unemployed. As a consequence, he had no capability to support his grandmother.

An incident occurred. The old woman became seriously ill. Owing to respiratory problem and high blood pressure she lost all her working ability. When there was none at home, the daughter-in-law took her motherland to a desolate railway station. When the grandson Radhamadhab arrived home, he enquired of his grandmother. His mother told, "I don't know where she has gone." Her son became angry and left the house to look for his grandmother. How pathetic it was! Radhamadhab found that his grandmother was lying dead on the railway platform. It was far from his residence. He hit upon a plan. It was bitting cold outside. Radhamadhab was bold by nature.

His conscience bothered much. He had only five rupees with him. Taking the corpse of his grandmother, on the shoulder he moved towards his home on feet. The ferry service was closed. At the dead of night requesting

the ferryman he took her home for the last time bearing
with agony. It might be the demise of the old woman was
a relief to all. Finally, the rituals of cremation were done.
What a tragic end !

CHAPTER FOUR

A Father's Sacrifice

That was at the dead of night. The elder son, Suman drank to the dregs. He said, "Open the door." Mother remained silent after opening the door. Mr. Das was a very good man by nature. He was truly a gentle man. He was a service holder. He had a sweet voice of singing. He knew how to play on the 'Tabla'. Such a good man sacrificed his all to the cause of his family. The man's wife whose name was Madhu loved him a lot. They had two sons. Both were handsome. But their characters were too loose.

The elder son failed in the Higher Secondary Examination. But he was not accustomed to good habits. Father sent him to Mumbai in search of a job. But he returned. He did not pay attention to any work steadily. No doubt the boy had some qualities. The boy's handwriting was excellent. He could draw well. He knew how to drive a car.

But the main fault in his character was to gossip with the naughty boys. He became addicted to gambling and smoking. He used to go to different places with ladies to have an affair which was not lawful. As his father was a serviceman, he had no financial obligation. But the situation became worse when his father superannauated from his service. His father had a shop also. Everything went wrong when the son became a drunkard finally.

Some people of the adjoining areas convinced his father that his son would be okay after the marriage. Thus, father decided to get him wedded. Suman agreed to the proposal of marriage. The family of Suman was also dependent on his father.

The father was blessed with his grandson. But conflicts went on. One day Suman came late at night. He got injured. His mother asked, "How has this taken place?"

Then he informed his mother that a neighbouring boy hit him badly when a quarrel occurred regarding the exchange of money.

This sort of activities of his son hurt the father immemsely. Gradually, his younger brother screamed and he was unemployed. He started to quarrel with his elder brother. It took a severe turn. Father tried to understand both his sons. But they turned deaf ear to his father's advice. The father was surprised at this behaviour of his sons. His daughter-in-law tolerated much. But there was the limit to be restrained. Then she decided not to stay here. His father-in-law heavy shocked. Her father-in-law was suffering from high blood preasure & sugar. Both the sons became more quarrelsome. There was no peace in the family although there was no crisis of money. The father erected a well-built house. But his elder son said one day, "I'll not dwell here any more."

"Why ?" said his father.

The father's plight was pathetic. Both his sons got separated. The father lost his temper and the power of endurance. One day it was biting cold outside. The father

was watching T.V. But he felt pain in his chest. He was
sent to the hospital. But on the way, he expired. What a
relief ! He got after his demise. His sacrifice to the cause of
the family came to an end.

CHAPTER FIVE

THE CONSCIENCE PRICKS

"As you sow, so shall you reap" – so goes the proverb in English. There was a man. His name was Basudev Sikder. He dwelt in a small town. He used to repair radios, TV, Electric gadgets and so on.

It was a summer day. A customer came to Basubabu's shop to repair a Television set. The defect was minor. But the man imposed high hike for the repair of the TV. The customer was innocent. He did not know the detailed history of the repaired TV. The customer was not affluent. Yet he paid for the demand done by Basubabu. It was not an act of honesty of Basubabu. However, the customer left the place and went home without any bargaining. It was a late evening. On that very day an occurrence took place.

Basubabu was not alone at home at that time. His wife, Sumana was sleeping. All on a sudden, the fans of the rooms stopped moving. The day was too hot to tolerate. Then his wife woke up and said, "Is anything wrong?" Basubabu said, "Perhaps loadshedding has happened." But it was found that there was no electricity in his house.

Basubabu was astonished. What the cause might be!

Basubabu told his wife, "Fetch me the matches." As he was a technician, he had a sound knowledge of electric matter. Finally, he discovered that all the lights were fused and the coils of the fans were burnt. His wife expressed her grudge over the incident. At that night both had to spend sitting outside the window of their home. When morning came, Basubabu had to call in an eletrician who charged heavily for the repair of the fans. Moreover, Basubabu had to purchase some new electric bulbs.

In a conversation with his tenant Basubabu shared the incident. Then the tenant informed him that it might be the fraud which he had done when he demanded a high price for the repair of the TV of a poorman.

At last, Basubabu realised what his fault was. So it was the pricks of conscience for which Basubabu regretted a lot. From that day, he learnt a good lesson. He thought of a plan that he would never cheat anybody anymore.

CHAPTER SIX

THE BENEVOLENCE OF A MISER

A man lived in a small old town. He had a son. The name of the son was Bibhuti Pal. Though the man was illiterate, he took care of his son's education deeply. The son was good at sports. He was also meritorious. By dint of his perseverance and tenacity, he carried on his higher studies. He never neglected his studies. Bibhuti's father was an amiable person. He devoted his entire life to the cause of his family. He loved his wife Sarala very much. In this way, the days passed by.

When the school final result was published, it was seen that Bibhuti had scored 99 out of 100 in Maths. He did well in the Science subjects. So, he chose the science stream to continue his further studies. From a neighbour he got an information regarding the admission to a Engineering College. He was admitted to a college of Engineering. Thus, he excelled in studies. He became a mechanical Engineer with high grades. He was lucky enough as he got employment in the Indian Railways after he had passed out.

Such a man was found rare. He was benevolent by nature. He was a very good human being. He never had a conflict with anybody. He was calm and a good tempered person. He never grumbled over anything. He used to assist his relatives whenever required. It might be in the matter of marriage or medication.

Once a relative name Paltu came to him. He was not afflent. He said, "Dada, help me, my daughter is going to be wedded. Instantly, he gladly accepted the proposal. He told Paltu "I will give my niece cot made of teak wood and a gold necklace".

Another incident would startle the readers. One of his relatives contacted him over phone. The relative told that his father-in-law was suffering from cardiac problem. He had savings certificates and also ornaments of gold and diamond. But at present he was very busy with the patient. Hearing this, he came home to the house of relatives taking one lac rupee without any terms and conditions.

Bibhuti was married to a beautiful girl whose dealings with other were very good. They had a daughter. The daughter was also very witty. With help of her father and her own intelligence she became a Government officer later on.

But the fact was that this merciful man was a miser by nature. He never wore good garments. He had no fascination for delicious food items. But he never deprived his family of that. He often used to go to set out for family tour. He avoided luxury at any cost. He donated if people came to him for financial help. He never took part in active politics. His only meditation was to help the destitute. Really, our society needs such a good man for the upliftment of the nation. The Almighty must bless him as he also looked after his own parents as well.

A GLOOMY TALE OF A HARLOT

Once a lass lived in an infamous countryside. She used to live with her parents. Her parents were needy. They had six daughters. Her father was too poor to assist. The daughters of the poor parents had no sufficient formal education. The father of the six daughters had no farming land. He used to work in a shop. His salary was not up to the mark. As a consequence, his family had to pass a time of hardship.

Years spent. The elder daughter named Soma, grew as an adult girl. Her father tried several times to get her married. But owing to lack of money, he failed to get her married. His elder daughter was lovely to look at. The eyes were splendid. But she was unlucky. She had to work was a maid servant in a palace. Everyone used to look down upon her. She helped her father in distress.By chance, an incident took place. The son of the richman what the girl worked used to rape her day after day promising the proposal of wedding. The innocent girl dreamt of a family. One day, being drunken the man of the rich man beat her ruthlessly. She was forced to live the work as a maid servant there. She was pregnant. This news spread like a blaze. The girl tried to hurt herself. At last, she left her father's cottage in disgust and in insult.

A local broker sold her to a brothel. There started another life of torture. Now she became a prostitute unwillingly. She never had a family. She never got any love in life. She had to execute the orders of the head of brothel passively. Her dream became empty. One day Soma told the tale of her tragedy to a customer. The customer enjoyed her sweet company. Soma said, "Babu, visit again." The babu gave her a lot of money. He took her to a hotel. The babu said, "Why have you come to this heinous profession?" The harlot replied, "I have six sisters. Who will marry them as my father is not rich to get them married."

Soma was the harlot whose only intention was to entertain the customers. None knew that he she had had a mind also. The babu was wondered to know the tragic story of the girl. She was really beautiful but she had no formal education. So she lost her dignity instead of her physical beauty. Her toil knew no bounds. When she was suffering for ailment, she had no substitute but to entertain her customer. She had no sons or daugthers. She was a living entity of mercilessness.

Really, she deserved the empathy of all. Days after days she had to face such brutal torture leaving her kith and kin. One day, it was found that her dead body was lying on the floor in a confined room. Now, who will look into the cause of her demise ? Perhaps, none noticed it. In this way, the gloomy story of a harlot came to an end.

CHAPTER EIGHT

ON THE TOP OF A ROOF

For the last sixty years there lived a man with his infirm mother. His mother was the lady of five sons. The four sons died before his mother's demise. The family was affluent. The Duttas were the reputed family of the vicinity. Nikhilesh Dey was the head of the family. After completing his graduation from Kolkata, he carried on his family business.

He was married to a lady. Their wedding was not an arranged one. They were a happy couple. A son was born to them. They reared the son whose name was Kamalesh with affection. He became an adult man step by step. He was not well at studies. Any way he passed B.Com in Accountancy.

His son mixed with evil company. He did not pay heed to his father's advice. In this way, he became rude. He did not want to do any work. He was plump. They had a lot of riches. His father was convinced by some well-wishers that the boy would not go to astray if he was wedded to any lady.

Oneday Kamalesh's father said, "Do you want to marry ?" The boy answered, "Certainly."

Then a 'bridal feast' was given. A lot of invitees were invited. As if, it was a gala festivity. The boy was happy with his wife. Years went on and went on. Father Nikhilish hoped that he would be the grandfather. He would play with his grand son and grand daughter. By the by the mother of Kamalesh became the patient of Perkinson. She could not walk. She sank on the chair. A care taker used to look after his ailing mother. The daughter-in-law

of Nikhilish Babu could not conceive. They were really unfortunate. Yet, they spent their life comfortably.

As Kamalesh was unemployed, he was suffering from high blood presure, sugar etc. As he had no child, his wife also unhappy. Still his wife did all the household works, whole heartedly.

Nikhileshbabu realised how the family would run after his death. Nikhilbabu was 76 years old. His wife could not do nothing. Her solace was that confined chair. She also spent time silently. Springs in her life were meaningless. What a grief ! She could not rejoice her life. She wept bitterly to the Almighty to snatch away her life.

What an alarming news came one day! His only son Kamalesh said, "I feel pain, papa." He was sent a local hospital. Unfortunately Kamalesh died on the way to the hospital due to cardiac arrest.

When the parents heard the news, they fainted. It was their turn to pass away. But their only son Kamalesh met with sudden attack on the heart living his wife and his old helpless parents.

What a pathetic news! Since then, the family was suffering from the plight of agony. They had no scarcity of wealth. But what they lacked in, they had no warmth. They had no grand son and grand daughter. Kamalesh passed away at the age of 49 creating a void in the family. On the top of a roof, there reigned hollowness.

CHAPTER NINE

THE ARROGANCE OF A FOP

The day was hot. The time was at night. All on a sudden, an angry driver entered into the bazar to look for a man who kept his bike on the side of a road. The driver of the four wheeler was too rude to describe. The driver who was in rage said, "Who kept the bike here? Have you no sense?" The streets were narrow and conjested. The owner of the bike turned up immediately. He said "What has happened?" The driver of the car was like a ruffian. He boldly and arrogantly said, "My intention was to smash the bike." The owner of the two wheeler was very innocent to look at. At the very moment he was about to purchase some vegetables. Hearing the clamour, he came and placed his bike properly.

I was the eye-witness of the incident which seemed to me utterly ridiculous. The owner of the bike never argued. He said, "I have kept it just now." The conduct of the driver of the four wheeler was too bad. He said, "Where have you been before coming to this reputed town?"

I was taken aback by the scenario. A gentle man
above the age of sixty was boast of his dwelling in the
city. He bluntly said, "That's means i.e. the owner of the
bike belongs to Midnapur." I don't know what logic is
behind this. That fop behaved as it he was too educated. I
thought, "This fop is a person whose glory for the city
was in vain." He was the man of false pride. He said, "This
is my town."

The man may be a victim of provincialism. He was
narrow-minded. He was tall and handsome. But his
character was too loose. Such a fop stood by the side of
the driver of the four wheeler. A man might be mistaken.
He was also ashamed of his deed. He felt extremely sorry
for the loss of that person's precious time for the driver.
But it was astonishing that he remained busy with the
scolding.

I was a mute spectator of the occurrence. A
flowervendor
was there. He also understood everything. The
boastfulness of the town was no place in a civilized society.
An illiterate person was capable of the nuisance they
created. Finally, the fop left the place as it he was a victor
and the driver drove the car in a hurry. Sometimes I
wondered, "What a place!" We all know that a person
shifts his own native place due to the change of workplace.
The dweller of the town had no empathy and co-operation.
I said, "They are just self centred." Such sort
of poeple are the disgrace to the nation as they were the
victim of the provincialism and false pride. We should
protest the hypocrisy of such kind of masses for the up
liftment of the society to a great extent.

They have no identity. Sympathy is meaningless in
the dictionary of the arrogant people. I sometimes became

nostalgic to see such inferior instances. No doubt, the city
is lovely. Is it lifeless?

CHAPTER TEN

AT THE CAFÉ

It was evening then and the day was hot. Kunal, a man aged 45 entered into the cafe to have some snacks. Kunal observed the incident that a man around sixty sitting on the sofa bending onto the shoulder of a young girl whose age seemed around twenty. Kunal was startled to hear from the whispers that they were engaged. The man questioned, "How have you enjoyed today, darling?" The girl did not pay any attention to the man's question. The girl said, "I need twenty thousand the next day." The man told her, "Yesterday I gave you fifteen thousand."

Then Kunal left for his own shop. He was busy with his work. His shop was near the railway station. He was habituated to the scenes that the girls of colleges and university smoke in front of him without hesitation. He thought, "Gone are those days." Sometimes he could not accept the degradation of the society he left.

After sometime, coming out of his shop, he was taking tea. He could not agree to the proposal and could not trust his ears. The two girls were approaching him and said, "Dada, we need some money." Kunal said, "What can I do for that?" One of the girls said, " Please relax and have sex." He innocently said, "Are you university students?" Then one of the girls commented, "Ours is a rich family. Father sends us at least twenty thousand rupees per month to bear with the educational expenses and others." They came of a rich family. Not only that, they were beautiful to look at and their faces were so charming that anybody might be captivated.

Then Kunal continued to gossip with them. They said, "We use branded garments, costly perfumes and we often visit to several restaurants with the boyfriends. But most of the boyfriends don't spend for us. We also assist them. So, we are in urgent necessity of money." The girls were impressed by the get up of his shop and by the beauty and appearance of Kunal, too.

Suddenly, rains started. They entered into the shop of Kunal not to get drenched.

Inquisitively Kunal asked, "How much do you need?" One of the girls said, "Only Rupees four thousand, please enjoy with us in too separate dates."

Then Kunal remembered the faces of his beloved wife and his adorable daughter. After that Kunal became speechless. Though he had an intention to do something i.e. sex, his ethics prinched him. He restrained himself. Next, showing no interest in the unexpected and incredible proposal of the girls, he nodded to the consent of his conscience. Then he left that place. He said, "What a society, we are leading today!"

As he is against the moral degradation, he could not devote himself to the illicit proposal given by two fair ladies.

CHAPTER ELEVEN

AN OPTIMISTIC OUTLOOK

How time passes by! Some memories torture us, some enthral us. But memories are mere memories. I want to relish such a memory that took place a few years back. Experiences teach us — is perfectly true. This experience is significant in my life as it moulds the shape of my own personality. This memory is so precious. That it helps in shaping my point of opinion. It has changed me a lot. I have gathered an emotional attachment. Some may differ from my view.

Before purchasing a flat of my own I had to dwell in different places by taking rented houses. Though we had a pucca building, we had to live in a rented house because of the distance of my service.

Now let me share an event that moved me very much. "Experience is the best teacher" proves again. One day, I set out for an evening walk. There were my son, Sovan and my wife, Lipika along with me. My son was cycling in the street. I saw that a family with whom we had a great connection was shifting their goods and luggage to a new place. The family used to live in our same colony.

When the commodities were being packed, they were standing outside. They said, "We have bought a flat in Kolkata. So, we are going to settle there." Their family consisted of three members. The man, his wife and their son aged six years lived. They happily without any obstacle. Oneday we met them, we felt morose. Very often the man and I walked on foot to go to the nearest market. They often came to our house. They were very friendly to us. They exchanged their new contact numbers and the address of the newly bought appartment. His wife gossiped and many more. Whenever they came to see me, he gave a sweet smile. Their tiny boy was very cute.

One day I became shocked to know a tragic incident that occurred unfortunately. We have not seen them for many days. Their mobiles were switched off. The other day I visited Kolkata and I asked a person of their apartment about them. He stood motionless for a while. After that, he informed me that cruel death had snatched the lives of the parents of that tiny boy. I said, "What a pathetic news!" I asked him how this happened. Then he told me that they passed away in an accident. Their son was at home. On thearing this, my whole family was stunned. Really, it was a sad event. I asked the person about the child. He said, "His relative has sent him to an orphanage." I thought to come across him. I went to the orphanage. I looked for him. They said, "The boy is in the garden." I saw him playing in the garden with other kids. When I came in close contact with him, he gave me that sweet smile forgetting his all pains.

I was perplexed at this event. He never thought that he has no future. After the great loss the child kept smiling. I said to myself, "Why cann't we smile like him?"

I have belief in the Almighty. Since then, I try to forget the frustration for my upcoming life. It has shaped my personality. So, I have an optimistic outlook and I expect for the best to take place.

29

CHAPTER TWELVE

BONDS OF AFFECTION

Still I cherish those days of my infancy and boyhood. Whenever I ran up to my grandmother, she threw her arms around my neck. I, too, used to feel elated at her affinity. She also seemed to be very cheerful to see me. Such was the bond of affection between my grandmother and myself.

My grandmother whose name was Chapala Pal was a very pious lady. I used to listen to the stories told by her. She was born in Faridpur, Bangladesh (now). She had six sisters and an elder brother. After the partition in 1947, their family came to India. She was married to Kalipada Pal at an early age.

I was the first son of her elder son Subodh Chandra Pal. I always clung to her. I could remember the days when I used to pluck flowers for the worship. She never scolded me. She had a special attraction for me.

My grandmother did not like to involve in domestic activities. She used to go to the temples located at various parts of Nabadwip. She preferred to sing and listen to devotional songs i.e. 'Kirtan' and she always attended devotional preachings like 'Bhagavat Patha'.

She used to bathe in the river holy Ganges everyday.

Whenever she used to visit temples, I insisted on going with her. Oneday, she said, "I will go now." I said "I'll go with you."

I recalled an incident. One of the ladies commented, "Is he your son?" My grandmother said, "No, she proudly declares me as her grandson."

I remember another event. I had been suffering from fever for a week. She wept piteously and she prayed to Lord Krishna to recover me soon. She always chanted 'Jay Nitai' in her lips.

Oneday I insisted on going with her, My father asserted, "My son would not be able to carry on his studies owing to over indulgence." Was this fact proved?

Years rolled by. She also grew old. My grandmother became wrinkled but her curly locks were not grey. She had a slender figure. Her only obsession was that after going outside she must change her clothing. I also was habituated to it.

Whenever, she found time, she used to count the beads of rosary. My friendship was deep-rooted. But this attachment turned a new twist. When my uncle bought a two-storied house at Chunchura, she went there with her younger son. In the meantime I got a govt. job, I settled to stay at Kalyani. This bonding was going to split little by little. Whenever I visited my hometown, she came to send me off. She blessed me silently.

Oneday my uncle informed me, that my grandmother had a high blood pressure. My grandmother disliked hospitals. She never had a wish to swallow bitter tablets. When she fell in, I went to visit her with my wife and son. Once she came to my place. I was fortunate enough.

A few months later, she faced cardiac problems. She was admited to the railway hospital in Kolkata. Where she breathed her last on 19th February, 2009. Thus, she left us quietly. As if I was in the void of loneliness. And my bonds of affection tore off. Her memories are still vivid and will remain for the days ahead. When my uncle rang me up in the early morning, "Your grandmother is no more." I was speechless. After listening to this sad news of her demise, I rushed to Nabadwip where her last furenal rites were performed.

CHAPTER THIRTEEN

AS IF IT WERE A GHOST!

The streets were lonely. It was midnight. It was a moonlit night. A man named Nirban was returning home from a bridal feast of his friends. His tiny daughter aged seven accompanied him. The daughter's name was Tiyasha. Her heart filled with immense delight. He was leaping like a mare.

Perhaps it was 2014. He was in Kolkata. When he was comming back, he was alone. When he was approaching towards his house, he stopped. "Why have you stopped here, Papa?" said the small girl. Nirban gazed at a tree far from him. He grasped his mobile phone and his daughter. He asked, "Who is there?" Then no reply came. He stood motionless and could not make up his mind.

Then his tiny girl, Tiyasha said, "What has taken place, father?" He told his daugher that he had seen a woman putting on a white sari on that tree. The girl started to cry in panic. Father said, "It may be a ghost on the tree."

Then the man had an idea. He switched on the light of his mobile phone. Then he moved silently. He flashed the light in all directions. None was found by him. He kept towards that tree. He observed, "A white sari was hanging from the tree. It was hanging as if a woman wearing white sari was there. Then he understood everything. He explained his daughter about such eventuality. As his fear was gone, he proceeded on with his small daughter, Tiyasha." Tiyasha jumped in pleasure. She sprang to his father's feet. There after, they set out for home. The thought of an imaginary ghost was gone.

Father and his daughter reached home slowly. Their palpitation was gone. Nirban described the entire episode to his beloved wife. His wife said, "You are a timid person." His wife boldly said, "I am not scared of ghosts." At that very night, Nirban could not have a sound sleep. He ordered his wife to close all the doors and windows properly. He went to bed chanting, "Rama, Rama." Perhaps his wife was correct to justify that Nirban had been a timid person. Getting up from bed at dawn, he took a vow that he would never go outside at the dead of night. What a man!

CHAPTER FOURTEEN

A MARRIAGEABLE DAUGHTER

Perhaps all must admit, "Marriage is one of the hallmarks of social positions." Sunilbabu used to live in a small town. He had a daughter whose name was Sarala. The girl was brought up with affection. She also did M.A. degree in Visual Arts. Her handwriting was excellent. Everything was going on smoothly. Years passed by. Now Sarala was 22 years old. In fact, she was eligible for the marriage.

Here a question arose. For the arranged wedding the girl used to sit before the proposed bride grooms and their kith and kin. The daughter of the girl, Sunilbabu once said to an old man who lived next door, "My daughter's complexion is black. Moreover, she is deaf. The old man wondered, "Is your daughter deaf ?" I am unable to trace it." Sunilbabu also stated, "Many a man comes and goes. No one comes with the proposal of marriage." The old man said, "No doubt your daughter's facial beauty is unique. Okay, I will try to help you in this matter."

Sunilbabu regretted, "My dream is to going to die. What can I do now?"

"Deafness is not a disgrace." said the oldman. The old man urged Sunilbabu not to worry over it.

The girl was lively. All the people loved her. But it was unfortunate that none came forward with the proposal of marriage. Sunilbabu could not ventilate his feelings to anybody except the oldman who was a well wisher of his family. All the men came to see and never turned up. Instead of her education, none proposed her to marry. The daughter of Sunilbabu felt insulted at this.

One day, she told her father, "I'll not sit on the 'bridal pidi' to marry." She further asked, "Am I a burden, father?" Her father also became restless and impatient for such a rejection by the men who only look at the outward beauty of a spinster. Sunilbabu cursed the society. He alleged, "Girls should be fair in complexion. Other wise, it has no worth in the eyes of fiance." The girl became a victim of pessimism. She thought her life was like a vacant infertile land. Her state of mind was not good. She considered her to be unlucky. She spent her days only drawing and by listening to sad music.

A change appeared unexpectly. That old man came with a bachelor and his parents. That bachelor said, "What's your name?" Due to deafness, the girl remained silent. Then that old man said, "Loudly asked the girl's name ? He further said, "Why are you so shy?" Then the girl responded. That oldman helped her to hear the questions raised by the bachelor and his parents."

Finally, that marriagle daughter of Sunilbabu tied the knot of bond. Her marriage became a grand success. The girl was able to captivate anybodies love by dint of her sweet behaviour. A few months went on. The girl became pregnant. She gave birth to a cute son. Her happiness knows no bounds. All the family members of

the newly wedded girl's-in-laws became elated. In this
way, Sunilbabu spent the remaining part of his life in glee.

37

CHAPTER FIFTEEN

WITH A LIMP

That was a summer day. But after the heat wave the atmosphere became lovely. As the unexpected shower made the people cheerful, the children as well as the aged persons all got some relief from the scorching heat of the sun.

A boy of thirty named Kanu Banerjee was a lame person. Though he was a B.Sc. (Hons.), he was unemployed. On that rainy day he was sitting alone on the road in a wheel chair. He was quitely quenched. At that time, a neighbour called, "Kanu, come." Kanu said, "I am in a hurry." Then the neighbour said, "Where will you want to go, Kanu?" He said, "I have to buy some necessary things. The neighbour said, "Go to your brother to bring those things for you." Kanu said, "They are too involved in domestic affairs. They have no time for me." Then he expressed his sorrow, "Though I am a graduate, I am a crippled person. I seek a govt. job. But still I am trying my best to get that job."

Then the daughter of neighbour Mrittika was highly qualified. He was also appearing at the various competitive examinations to get employed. Then she suggested, "Uncle, read the employment news. Get prepared for the

examination. She also asserted, "Uncle you have an extra
chance because of your physical deformaties."

Kanu listened to the suggestion of the girl, Mrittika
with rapt attention. Kanu was engaged in private tuition
for eight years. He used to live with his elder brother and
his family.

From that day, Kanu took an oath to get a Govt.
job. Then there conversation was continuing. The
neighbour said, "Now marry." His head nodded.

This lame man once proposed a lady who was
unwlling to marry him as his work was not permanent.
With broken heart with the limp he struggled for the
fortune
ahead. This man Kanu was humble by nature and
softspoken.
He could work a lot. His energy was indomitable.
So, achievement knocked at his door. He was brilliant.
His knowledge on science was like the vast sea.

A year later he got a govt. job. He became a clerk
in a Govt. office. His life became secured. Now it was the
turn of wheel in his life.

Now many fathers of bride were approaching with
the marriage proposal. Some once chose him as the eligible
man. He was wedded to a lady who turned to support him
in the coming days. They had a beautiful daughter called
Sujata. In this manner, a man with a limp became
successful in the battle of life.

CHAPTER SIXTEEN

WHAT A LAME LOGIC!

One day in the evening two plump women got down from a toto. The driver of the toto claimed Rs. 20/- as fare in addition to what the women had given. The riders of the Toto were two women and four children. The crux of the whole conflict was over the fares of the children which the toto driver demanded.

A passer by was on the road. He saw the scenario. When the two large women got down from the toto, one of the woman said, "Take your fare." She gave the toto driver Rs. 20/- as per head. Then the toto-dirver asked, "Will you not give me Rs. 20/- as the fair of the children?" Thus the dispute arose. The passer by was astonished at the reasons provided by the two women. They collectively started to attack verbally on the toto driver. The dresses of the women were pompous. They apparently look to be elite. But their reasons were illogical.

One of the women asserted, "After five years the fare for the children may be given."

How qualifed was the toto driver was unknown. But the way he tackled the matter deserved to be appreciated.

The toto driver said, "If the child is one, it is okay." Then I could not demand. The fact was that four children were occupying the seats. If any passenger was supposed to turn up, the toto driver had no option but to deny.

The women again gave the same logic. She said, "I will not pay extra fair." The toto driver said, "In case of bus fair above three years the fair is chargeable." He further said, In case of trains to take a bath full fare is to be paid." He also said, "In case of air flight, an infant's fair is chargeable."

The women got bewildered to listen to the logic given by the toto driver. The toto driver said, "Please stop". The passer-by was sighing that we are so miser to give justified money to a person who is needy. He also startled at the comment passed by the two large women. He left the place saying, "What a lame logic given by the two women in comparison to the logic given by that poor toto driver."

CHAPTER SEVENTEEN

THE BALLOON-SELLER AND HIS FATE

It was a sunny day. A boy was standing on the road with a pole where various colour of balloons were hanging. Sweat was falling from his forehead. He was thirsty. He had a wish to buy coconut water. But it was beyond his capability. He could not bear with the scorching heat of the sun. He came out from his house to sell balloons in order to support his family.

The boy seemed sixteen or seventeen years judging by his face. All on a sudden, the boy started to cry. A passer-by was going there. The passer-by asked, "What's your name?" The boy said, "I am Pratap."

Then the boy cotinued to tell his sad tale. He informed the man that his father had died a week ago due to the heat wave. His father was the victim of the sun stoke. The other days father was in tensed mood as he was jobless. The boy also asserted that he had passed the M.P. Exam. He had an aspiration to go on his studies.

The passer–by said, "How many members have you in your family?" The boy said, "I have my mother and the little sister." Then the man said to him, "I have my mother and a little sister." Then the man said to him, "Why are we crying bitterly?" He said, "I am trying to sell these balloons." They are of no use. None is coming to purchase. I am helpless. I don't know how I will stand by my family. I've to purchase milk for my little sister. Mother's mental condition is not good. Then she is, too, crying because she has lost my beloved father, of late."

The man was a business man. He was good at heart. He promised to give a job for the boy so that he could support his family without any hesitation. Then the man was so benevolent that often used to visit their house and helped a lot. The boy again decided to continue his higher studies as he got a job for night shift. Thus, the family started to move from that unexpected blow i.e. the death of his father of the teeneger.

The teeneger proved himself to be successful as he had a dream. That benevolent man said, "If one can strive, if one has a planning, he must achieve and shine in life." This proved once again in the case of this boy. So goes the proverb, "Man is the architect of his own fate". In future, this teenager became a businessman and did his M.B.A. From that, balloon seller how his story will inspire all for the generations to come.

CHAPTER EIGHTEEN

THE STORY OF FIVE INCHES

Far away from the town there lived a man in the country side. The man used to till the lands of his own. But he was not cheerful at heart. The man also had a farming house. The man was married. Once the man used to regret, "I have no child, although I have much wealth." Then one of his relatives told him not to worry. He said to the cultivator, "Have faith in the Almighty."

A few years passed. A good news spread. The wife of the peasant named Sulata became pregnant. The farmer was so elated that he started to distribute a lot of sweets among the villagers.

Finally, a new born baby saw the light. All of the villagers were astonished at the size of the baby. It was a stange baby, whose size was five inches. After the day of birth, that peculiar child started talking. All know, "Generally a baby cannot talk after its birth." It took place miraculously. Many a man assembled the peasant's house to see the baby. Its height, weight, size everything stunned the people greatly.

After very day of birth, the baby said to his father, "Father, I will go with you for cultivation." His father became speechless. What a talk it was! But the father of the baby didn't agree on this point. He told his son, "You are too tiny to do that kind of work." But the baby insisted on going with his father. His father became puzzled. He could not make up his mind what to do now. Then one day he decided to take his small baby to the green field.

When his father consented, the baby became glad like a free bird. The peasant took his baby and kept him under the cool shade of a nearby tree. All on a sudden, the peasant found his sound missing from there. He was so perturbed.

At that very time the baby said, "I am here." Then the man again was busy with his tilling work. Again he found that the baby was not there.

That tiny boy of five inches went on to chase the oxen so as to cultivate the land. The peasant went on to look for the boy. The man could not find him. Then the baby said, "I am here." Actually he was not found because the baby was under the cowdung. At that moment, a gang of burglars discovered the baby from the cowdung. They were thrilled to know that this baby was endowed with many capabilities. This tiny child was so cunning to befool anybody.

The leader of the thieves thought of a plan. The leader of the gang took the cunning and strange baby and he wanted to steal the baby to still from others' houses.

One day, at midnight the thieves took the baby with them. They convinced the baby to steal. The baby entered into the hole of the window of the hour of a rice man.

That baby hit upon a plan to make the thieves caught. One night the baby sat on the breast of a rich man. The baby tried, "Thief, thief." The man woke up from his sleep and found nothing. The rich man thought that it might be a dream. Then the man heard the same cry, "Thief, thief." Then he detected this tiny baby and the tiny baby disclosed all the matter regarding burglary to the rich man. In this way, the man caught the thieves with the help of this baby. This news spread like a violent storm.

The king was known to the fact. He rewarded this strange baby with lots of gold coins. Now the boy expressed his desire to meet his parents. The parents were informed of the whereabouts of this missing strange baby of five inches. The gloomy parents became happy with the reunion of thier son who was a unique kind.

CHAPTER NINETEEN

PEOPLE'S PROTEST

Suddenly I heard a hue and cry. I was on the road standing by. I was with my mother. I went to a town called Krishnanagar with a view to consult a physician. The town was busy at the peak hours.

I said, "We have always heard that ther are some persons who have a vomitting tendency while going on buses. It is a quite natural phenomenon that often chidren and women have a vomitting tendency."

But I have a strange experience in that town. I could not believe my eyes. I was stunned at this event that occurred a few years back. At that time I was probably a college student. The incident that took place shook me and I became amazed. And at that same time, I felt pity for the boy with whom the event centred round. A running bus stopped suddenly in front of me. The people who were the passengers of that bus, were getting down in rage. I said to my mother, "What is the cause of their anger?" I observed the scene minutely.

A teenaged boy started to vomit outside the window of that running bus. The remnants of the vomiting substance fell on the heads of three passers by. They became angry. They wanted to beat that boy whose father tried to convince them that he had done this because of his sickness. He begged pardon to them.

The passers-by said, "I have just left home to attend my job." The passengers of the bus watched that they had also been affected by the vomitting, "All became furious. The attendant and the driver of the bus also joined them. They demanded, "Give money to clean the bus." Thus a pandemonium was going on. Then the father of the boy repeatedly pleaded to stop this. At last it was decided that the ill boy would not be permited to travel by bus.

The father and the boy were forced to get down from the bus. They wanted to reach Kolkata by bus. Unfortunately, they could not reach their destination. Perhaps the next day, a strike was called. They were in perplexed condition. Then the decided to go to a house whose owner was luckily known to them. They took refuge in their hospitality for the time being. This scene moved me a lot.

CHAPTER TWENTY

A FAKE GHOST

There stood a man. He claimed himself to be a courageous
man. The name of the courageous man was Subir. He
bragged about his bravery always. He used to say, "I can
do everything."

One day one of his neighbours tried to testify to his
unreal vanity. It was the darkest evening of the year. It
was winter. It was dizzling now and then. Then that
neighbour hit upon a plan in order to test his courage.
This brave man not only declared himself as a brave person
but also looked upon others as timid ones. A change came.
The neighbour wanted to teach him a good lesson. He
asked, "Are you scared of ghosts?" Subir, the brave man
answered, "Never." Then the neighbour who clung to do
some mischief. He said to Subir, "Will you do a simple
work?" If you can, I promise to give you Rs. 20,000/-
after the work is over." The brave man said, "Okay."

Subir was also greedy. He got a victim of the
consequence. He said to his neighbour, "What should I
do now?"

The neighbour said, "Today is a chilly and a rainy night.
The burning ghat is desolate. I'll give you the promised the
money if you can do that. " Then the brave

man said, "Tell me, what I will do." The neighbour said to Subir, "Take this stick. You have to insert this stick into the earth of the burning ghat in the dead of night." Then Subir informed, "It is a candid job."

Then Subir said, "Let me do it." Then the neighbour gave him a big tall iron rod to insert into the soil of the burning ghat alone.

Subir took it as if he was very smart to do so. Subir left for the burning ghat with that mission wearing a shawl.

He reached the spot and there was none on the secluded spot in such a cold night. Now he attempted to put the stick into the core of the soil. At that very moment, his shawl also was inserted along with the stick. When he tried to stand erect, it seemed to him that someone held him behind.

He became nervous. Now he was thinking about the presence of the ghost in the chilly night. His bravery was gone. He got frightened. It was discovered next day that he was lying dead. Perhaps he died of the phobia of a fake ghost. How courageous he was!

CHAPTER TWENTY-ONE

A WEDDING JEOPARDY

Swapan and Swapna were like two characters of a novel. They lived in a small town in the district of North 24 Parganas. They had two sons whom they reared with intense care. Both of them were excellent in studies. Both were careful about their career. The names of Swapan babu son's were Sushil and Subimal.

The elder son of Swapan babu did his M.A. in History and M.A. in Education. After obtaining Ph.D. Sushil tried his best to opt for lectureship in a college. His brother, too was very brilliant. He passed M.Sc. in Maths. He got a service in a govt. bank. Subimal had a love affair with a local girl whose beauty was beyond description. They settled in Kolkata after the marriage was over.

But there was negative aspect in the case of Sushil. He got employment late when he was nearly thirty-five. He was almost crazy to get him wedded. His parents were too old. They had no intention to marry off Sushil. His brother already married his lady love. There was a suspicion in the minds of the parents of Sushil that if this son became married, he would also leave them alone like his younger brother.

His son, Sushil was tall, dark and handsome. He could not manage how to marry a damsel of his own. Then he became restless. Then he said to one of his colleagues, "I have informed the parents of the brides by calling your names." The colleague was innocent. He agreed to the proposal. He consented, "It's all right."

Suddenly, a phone call came to Sushil, the colleague of Sushil. He said, "Ride on my bike." Sunil said, "Where will you go?" Then he told Sunil, "Let's to go to my flat with me. The father and the brother of the bride have come to meet me."

Sunil said, "How did you contact, Sushil?" He said, "I have collected the contact number from the newspaper."

Sushil rushed to the shop of sweet-meats. Keeping Sumit alone to discuss with the strangers to talk to them until his return. As the age 35 was a crucial age, more ever, his brother had already settled. He was obstinate to do something. Sometimes, marriage proposals were in vain. After the meeting, they never came forward to proceed the matter of wedding further.

A wedding geopardy was continuing on. In fact the flower of marriage was yet to bloom.

Then came a beautiful proposal given by his relative to tie the knot. This family was noted for their name and fame. They chose this bridegroom and at last the marriage ceremony took place in a pompous way. Sushil's anxiety and perplexity vanished for ever.

CHAPTER TWENTY-TWO

A PECULIAR MAN

Oneday while I was going to Santipur by train, I met a strange man. It was a sudden meeting. As I was a daily passenger, I came across several people on the way to my house and on the way to my working place.

The person whom I met was old. He was an aged man. His age was nearly 70 years. It seemed to me. There were many people in the compartment. It was perhaps the time when the 'Rash Puja' festival was held at Santipur. This place is famous for the Rash Puja festival. During this time many people visit this sacred place.

Sometimes, we, the daily passengers, remain un aware of the events that take place in the running local train. I took a seat luckily by the window inspite of heavy crowd. I was busy to converse with my co-passengers who were also service-holders. Probably it was in the month of November when the incident was witnessed by me. We were chatting in the railway compartment. All on a sudden, an old man got in the compartment. He was a very comical man by nature. He began to converse with us. At that very moment, I heard the ringtone of a mobile phone. I tried to guess whose mobile was ringing. Bychance that old man stood. The ring tone stopped. Again, the same ringtone was heard. The old man bent again. I was surprised what the matter was. Then I followed the occurrence minutely. That old man was talking to a person. Then he stooped. I said, "Why are you stooping, uncle?"

After that, he showed, "Look here. There is a pocket at the bottom of his pant." I enquired, "What is this?" The old man said, "I keep my mobile phone into the pocket of my pant." I said, "Why, uncle?"

He tried to explain the causes for this. He said, "This prevents my mobile phone to get stolen." I got amazed.

Then he said, "I am conscious of my health. I am physically

fit even at this age. He said, "We should not keep the mobile phone either to the pocket of breast or to the pocket of abdomen. This will stop the radiation of mobile phones. I asked to myself, "Really, most of us though we know it, we don't abide by this." Then the man got down from the train. We started to discuss about this peculiar man. How concious he was! Truly, I never met such a person in my whole life. I think, this is a rare case."

CHAPTER TWENTY-THREE

THE EGOISTIC BEND OF MIND

A man or woman cann't be happy if not, he or she limits his or her aspiration. Anything excessive is not good. A right path has to be chosen. Once there lived a lady who was self-centred by nature. She was ill-tempered, too. She used to brag about her arrogance all the time. The lady's name was Arpita. She was a beautiful lady, no doubt.

She dwelt in a town in the district of Howrah. She was a typical lady. The entire family was anxious about her whimsicality and ego. When she was studying in a university, her family decided to get her daughter married. Her father said to his daughter, "Are you engaged?" The girl replied, "No". But she expressed her desire. She said, "I will agree to a proposal if you find out a wealthy bride groom".

The lady was greedy, too. Finally, she nodded. She was married to a reputed professor. His husband was contratry to her wife. He was considerate and calm. All on sudden, a conflict arose. She said to her husband, "I am not interested in staying in a joint family. At last, to avoid serious consequences, her husband took her in a rented house.

The newly wedded couple started to lead a happy conjugal life.

Then an adorable son was born to them. By the by, woman got a government service. The lady became busy with her new working place. One day her husband said, "Please pay heed to household works. Our child is too tiny." She furiously replied, "I am in haste, engage a cook." Her husband agreed on this point. It seemed, the lady was scared of domestic works.

One day an incident took place. The office was closed early. But she said, "I will not go home now." One of her colleagues replied, "Why?" She said, "If I go to house now, I have to wash the clothes myself."

Even she was boast of her beauty. She often told her colleagues, "My lips are kissable." I never wanted to marry such a man. All her colleagues tried to convince her. But she did not pay attention to their advice.

After a few years, she had an attack on heart. Thus, her health soon became deteriorated. Before her retirement she had to leave this mortal world leaving her old husband and her only son. Her son's name was Anurag. His studies went on. He had to settle abroad. But he did not look after the movement of his father. His father grew old. Though he was a pensioner, none came to assist him. He passed away at the dead of night oneday. Thus, owing to the egoistic bend of mind of a lady of family set up came to ruin.

CHAPTER TWENTY-FOUR

A MIGRANT LABOURER

One afternoon, a dark, tall, handsome man was standing on the pavement. His name was Tusharkanti Sarkar. He was an unskilled worker. He returned home from Chennai after a prolonged illness. He wedded his wife Shipra ten years ago. They had no child.

Oneday his wife said to husband, "Please stay here. "Don't go beyond my sight as it is the time of Lockdown".

The man said, "Exile in remote place is my fate." His wife repeatedly told me, "Different types of news are coming. It is a pandemic situation. Don't leave me alone."

He said to wife, "I have to earn, my beloved." His wife said, "There is a news that migrant workers are coming back home. All are in a deadly situation."

His husband said, "I have no relief. I have to go for my work. Don't think too much. I'll come again to fulfil our dream that will be blessed with an infant."

Saying this, the husband of Shipra went to work. He did not listen to the words of his wife.

By the by Shipra became worried. Various death news was coming from different corners of the country.

She remained silent. She remained deaf. She remained passive.

The very next day an urgent phone call came. She leapt to get the call. But how terrible the news was! Her husband left this mortal world leaving her alone. As if she was ready to die but the old parents of the daughter (Shipra) convinced her a lot. The lockdown once lifted. She could not see her husband for the last rituals. She was in distress. She was in mental dilemma. None came forward to give her solace except her old parents. No relatives stood by her. She was in darkness. All her cherished dreams to have a child were shattered. She had no where to go an except her parent's dilapidated home. To maintain the family and to make both ends meet Shipra started to sew garments. She worked day and night.

One day an old neighbour came to their house. "Where has your husband gone?" The mournful woman said, "He has gone to work for ever." The woman sighed "Don't shed tears. Be hard working. Think of yourself." The bereaved woman accepted the neighbour's sympathy calmly.

CHAPTER TWENTY-FIVE

A TRAGEDY OF A TALENT

One day the humidity was too unbearable. It was a day in summer. I could not tolerate the heat wave of the sun. I was sitting on a bench on the railway platfrom. The train which I caught was late. At that very moment, a young handsome boy sat beside me. He said to me, "Uncle, where will you go?" I said, "I have to consult an eye specialist."

Then a nice chatting went on with that handsome boy. What a shocking news! I listened to his tragedy with rapt attention. His old father was with him. At first his father could not understand who I was. His father was suffering from glaucoma. The young boy told me that he had gone to Chennai, Hyderbad but he had nothing to do. I said, "Why?"

He informed that he was an M.A. M.Phil in Education. He was busy with the father's treatment. He said, "His father may be blind oneday. He cann't read properly. Even he cann't sign his signature." I said, "It is really pathetic." I said to the young boy, "Have you no brother and sister?" The boy burst out into tears. He said,

"I am the only child of the family." He further stated that, his mother passed away last year. I said, "How do you maintain your family?" He said, "Our family depends upon my tuition which is the only income we have."

He said, "I used to sit for several competitive exams." But he further declared that he was not fortunate enough. He said, "I have no money to start a business. Moreover, he has none to look after his father." He regretted, "Who will marry an unemployed youth?" He continued his tale of sorrow. To hear it, I got shocked. He told me uncle perhaps a day would come when I have to sell my vital organ of body i.e. Kidney. He said, "I don't know farming. I don't know fishing, my dream has broken." My beloved has left me and she has wedded another man. He said, "Who will plant a tree in my barren land?" He said, "I am in distress." He said, "My life is the life of failure and frustration." I said, Don't give in to the destiny. Your days of adversity will reduce." Have faith in the Almighty. I said to the young boy, "Be determined and work hard. I believe your tragedy will be removed.

CHAPTER TWENTY-SIX

A TALE OF WOE

In a small town there lived a nice family. The family consisted of three members. The members lived quite gladly. There was a daughter whose name was Jhuma. She was a girl of beauty. His parents adored her very much.

The father of the daughter was a clerk in a Govt.-aided school. Her father's name was Narayan Das. His wife was also a fair lady. She was also very pious. The beautiful family used to live in a small house.

Years went by. The child grew up. She was so adorable. She loved her father and mother dearly. She completed her school education. Thereby it was the time of getting admission to a college. She was admitted to a nearby college. Thus, her studies went on.

But the two sudden events shake the happiness of the nice family. Narayanbabu is going to retire from his service soon. Then he had a plan that his daughter should be married off. One of his friends said, "Narayan, why do you want your daughter getting married soon." Narayan remained silent. Then the man started to weep bitterly infront of his friend who was his constant well-wisher. He said, "My liver is damaged." I may depart this mortal world any day. Thereafter, his friend Nirban said, "I agree to the proposal of yours." Then searching for the bridegroom started.

Some who nodded to wed. Some claimed huge dowry. Some denied because they would not marry a single daugher. Some of the persons were from far distance. Such causes hampered the sutdies of the daughter called Jhuma.

Her marriage was settled at last. The girl was compelled to stop her studies. A tale of woe began in this way. She was got wedded to an affluent family. The man was a merchant. Finally, It was established that the bridegroom was a divorcee. Then the conflict of the family started. The main crux of the dispute was that the man was habituated to wine. He was addicted heavily. Finally she began to torture upon the newly married wife. Suddenly the father of the daughter Jhuma passed away. It was the unexpected blow to the married lady. Jhuma was pregnant. She was sent to her parental house. She took birth to a son. But the fact was that, his husband was called in for several times. He never responded. The girl was totally helpless. She was unable to complete his studies again. Her mother became mentally imbalanced. Under such circumstances, Jhuma could not make up her mind what to do. She was puzzled. The family was dependent upon the meagre family pension. The girl had a dream that her son would become an established person in future. But she started to struggle.

She started medical treatment for her ailing mother. In course of time, her mother recovered soon. It was her only refuge. None looked after the fairness of Jhuma. In this world of sadness no well-wisher came forward to help her. Then she was involved in fashion designing as her profession. She fought and fought. Perhaps now, her tale of woe would diminish one day.

CHAPTER TWENTY-SEVEN

A COMICAL MAN

Many days have passed by. A man lived in a pucca building. His location was at Ranaghat, a Sub-divisional town in the district of Nadia. The name of that man was Mr. Subal Das. He was a teacher by profession. He was a very funny character. Everybody who came in contact with him was ammused at his hilarious behaviour. This emerged from his inner nature. He never blamed anybody. He never expressed his rage over his comical attitude.

This funny attitude of the teacher showed his simplicity. It was not his folly. He was a scholar. He did his M.A. in History from Rabindrabharati University. Actually, this teacher was not sad in his entire life. He used to live a happy life. There was financial stability to run his family.

His wife's name was Mira Das. She was also an honours graduate. She worked in a government office. They had a lovely daughter whose name was Mithu Das. What strikes everybody was that he was not at all serious. Subal babu took everything in a light hearted manner. Some of the occurrences show that he was a simple man. One day he attended a seminar of which he had no previous notion. Many a teacher joined that seminar. The very next day when he came to school, he said to himself, "I am a blockhead." One of his collegues asserted, "Why? Mr. Subal Babu." I know nothing about the seminar. But two foolish teachers sitting beside me, asked me an absurd question. He said, "What is the topic to be discussed in the Seminar?"

Oneday he disclosed his family matter openly. Subalbabu said, "I get down into the water tank." One of his colleagues commented "What happened after that?" Subalbabu said, I was unable to lift myself out of the water tank. Subalbabu was very fat and his height was too short. If someone were to fill the tank after switching on the motor, everyone began to laugh. Then some masons were engaged in his house to do some maintenance works. Subalbabu said, "Save me, I cann't get out of this water tank." At last, he was taken out of the water tank with the aid of the masons. Readers, imagine the situation.

Another incident amused all. Subalbabu was a patient of diabetes. But he was fond of sweets. Perhaps his wife, Mira forbade him to eat sweets. But whenever, chances appeared, he forgot his ailment. One day a picnic was arranged by his friends. One of his friends noticed an amusing thing. He said, "What are you doing Subalbabu?" His wife was also present in that feast.

Subalbabu became scared of seeing his wife approaching towards him. His mouth was full to the brim with 'Rosogolla'. His wife asked, "What is in your mouth?" His mouth was so full with sweets that at that very moment he was incapable of talking to his wife. Then he told her everything. She became angry. Then Subalbabu promised her not to touch sweets any more. Such were the few comical incidents of this innocent and candid person.

CHAPTER TWENTY-EIGHT

DON'T IGNORE ANYONE

All know that life is a mixture of weal and woe. Some may believe in destiny. "Man is the architect of his own fate"— is proved again.

A man used to live in a small town called Kanchrapara. He had his two sisters. Their names were Pratima and Suchitra. His father died suddenly. The man's name was Ashoke. His mother tried hard to bring him up. At that time the man did his bachelor degree with honours in Chemistry. That man struggle in the battle of life a lot.

Perhaps due to the lack of financial support he was unable to start a business. Perhaps he was a victim of politics. In a word, he was unable to get a government job. But he tried his best.

The man was married to a lady whose inspiration made him to the path of economic stability. Theirs was not an arranged marriage. But the marriage was based on pure love. They had a son and a daughter. There were four members of his family i.e. Ashoke, beloved mother, his wife and the two children. His mother used to get small family pension. Ashoke's wife started to input coaching as she did her master degree in Economics. Thus, the family ran in difficulty.

Another blow came unexpectedly when his mother passed away. She died from over-eating. Gone was the small pension of his mother. Then the man started a small business. One of his relatives suggested him to ply a Toto Rickshaw. No kith and kin assisted him with some money. But they gave him a lot of advices.

He felt ashamed. Then a friend proposed him to do something for him. He was a mechant. With the help of his friend, he dreamt a big dream. He used to toil day and night. His wife also earned a lot through tuition. Thus the fate of wheel moved on. Once upon a time this man's only means of communication was a bi-cycle. Whenever he visited nearby areas, he used his bi-cycle. Even his wife was forced to ride on it.

Now this Ashokebabu has become a millionaire. Oneday his uncle said, "What do you do now, Ashoke?" Ashoke said, Kaku, "I have a small business."

Actually the neighbours and his relatives were envy of him. One day he bought a motor bike. One of his neighbours said, "Have you borrowed money?" Ashoke politely responded, "No aunty, I have bought it in cash."

But all were astonished when he bought a four wheeler whose price was more than twenty lacs.

Once his own brother-in-law asked, "How much is the EMI, Ashoke?"

Ashoke replied and informed him modestly, "I pay income Tax more than three lacs per annum." Then his brother-in-law was speechless. He could not believe his ears. So by dint of stiff toil, Ashoke has achieved success in life. Hence, we should not ignore any one. None knew that Ashoke would be an enormously rich man.

LUCK SMILES UPON A LADY

Oneday a young lady was crying bitterly on the bank of a rivulet. An old man, Nirmalbabu was sitting by her. He asked, "What's your name? Where do you reside?" The young lady remained silent for a while. The old man was thoughtful of the fact that the lady might kill herself by drowning into the river.

Nirmalbabu was not a person who was not helpful. He again said to her, "What's your address?" The girl was lovely to look at. The lady was still crying. The old man tried to soothe her and he tried several times to know her name and residence. The oldman thought that the lady might be deaf. The cause of her crying was unknown to him. At last the oldman announced, "He is going to inform the police soon if she does not disclose her identity."

After a few seconds, the lady informed her that her name was Gita. Gita informed that she was married to an unemployed man by falling in love with him. But her husband often beats her. The lady said, "I want a baby". But her husband, Sabuj disagreed.

Gita continued to tell her sufferings in her father-in-law

law's house. The old man, Nirmalbabu said "This is
the cause of departure from your father in law's house.
"Yes", said the woman.

Then Nirmalbabu said to her, "What do you want
now?" Thereafter, the lady said, "I want to go to my
parents' house. "Where is it?" asked the oldman. The lady
said, "It is at a town located in the district of Hooghly."
The old man assured her that he would assist her to reach
her parents' house. Accompaning her the oldman arrived
at the destination by her parents' house by train.

From here another chapter of lady's life started.
The parents of the lady were poor. They were unable to
feed her. Her father was on the bed of demise. Her mother
quarrelled with her always. A few months later, her father
passed away. Then a brutal torture started on her. She
was confused. Her two brothers were young to do anything
for her.

Purchasing a sewing machine started to work day
and night to help the family in poorly financial condition.
One day a relative came to the house and the young lady
ventilated her grief to the relative. The relative was sure
that such a lady deserved to lead a stable life. Gita struggled
to survive in this sort of discrimination.

Oneday she dropped a plate made of glass. Her
brother rebuked her piteously. Now she thinks, I have no
place to go. Gita complained at her fate. She cursed her
parents.

Two years passed in this way. Then the relative of
the young lady approached their house. He said, "I have
a good news for you." Gita said, "I know the wounds of
my ill-fate." Then the relative narrated an incident that he

had faced recently. The relative used to live in the town of Kanchrapara. He was going to Kolkata by train. An unknown man sat beside him. He talked to the problem of servants. The unknown man said, "I have lost my wife. I have a son who lives in a foreign country." Now, I am in an urgent need of a maid servant. Then the relative of the young lady took the phone number from him. He told the unknown man that he would contact later on. The relative of the unknown man unfolded all the details to the murder of the young lady. Mother consented that her daughter might go to work leaving us.

A new chapter of lots of happiness started. Gita got all her luxuries. She lived in a three storied building like a queen. Now maidservants were engaged to look after her. The young lady was wedded to the rich man. They had a daughter. Now, she was able to help the poor condition of her mother and brothers. They frequently visited the house of Gita. Now it is proved finally that luck smiles upon the young lady.

A User of Slang Languages

There lived a unique man in a country side. He always used to use slang languages. The man's name was Raghu. Whenever he met people, he used slang languages. Whether it was in the company of gentlemen or uneducated folk, it was his common nature.

One day an invitation of marriage ceremony came to him. This marriage ceremony was the party of a reputed person. All his relatives were afraid of him because Raghu might use slang languages any time and anywhere. His wife Riya said, "You cannot attend this invitation. I am taking an oath not to use any bad words."

But the family members of Raghu are not sure of this false promises. Because they had a previous experience. Raghu used slang languages there. But Raghu insisted on going the wedding party.

It was decided that Raghu would be surrounded by a known person to make him cautious of the remarks. Raghu obeyed his nephew very much. He always listened to the advice given by him. His nephew followed his maternal uncle Raghu all the time. It was all right initially.

At last, that akward incident took place. Raghu was given delicious dish on the day of marriage ceremony. The father of the bride holding his hands folded approached Raghu. He asked Raghu, "How are the food items that served to you? Is everything fine?" Raghu remained silent for a while. Then Raghu shook his head to say that everything was okay. But the father of the bride was standing there still. This time, Raghu would not help but using slang languages. Raghu commented, "All are delicious. But the chatnee is so nasty using evil words."

The bride's father became wondered to listen to such words. He could not trust his ears. He burst out in shame and left the place. So, it was evident that none could regist Raghu from uttering such bad words. These words were the natural flow of Raghu. It was established that natural things are impossible to stop. It was the flow like the showers.